BLINK!

For Amy Rennert,
who helped me see so much
xo
—Amy

For my nephew Joel
—Uncle David

Text copyright © 2018 by Amy Krouse Rosenthal
Jacket art, interior illustrations, and hand lettering copyright © 2018 by David Roberts

All rights reserved. Published in the United States by Random House Children's Books,
a division of Penguin Random House LLC, New York.

Random House and the colophon are registered trademarks of Penguin Random House LLC.

Visit us on the Web! randomhousekids.com

Educators and librarians, for a variety of teaching tools,
visit us at RHTeachersLibrarians.com

Library of Congress Cataloging-in-Publication Data
Names: Rosenthal, Amy Krouse. | Roberts, David, illustrator.
Title: Don't blink! / by Amy Krouse Rosenthal ; illustrated by David Roberts.
Other titles: Do not blink!
Description: First edition. | New York : Random House, [2018] | Summary: "A page turns every time you blink,
bringing you closer to the end of the book—and bedtime." —Provided by publisher.
Identifiers: LCCN 2014026921 | ISBN 978-0-385-39187-0 (hardcover) |
ISBN 978-0-375-97364-2 (hardcover library binding) | ISBN 978-0-385-39188-7 (ebook)
Subjects: | CYAC: Bedtime—Fiction. | Books and reading—Fiction.
Classification: LCC PZ7.R719445 Do 2018 | DDC [E]—dc23

MANUFACTURED IN CHINA
10 9 8 7 6 5 4 3 2 1
First Edition

Random House Children's Books supports the
First Amendment and celebrates the right to read.

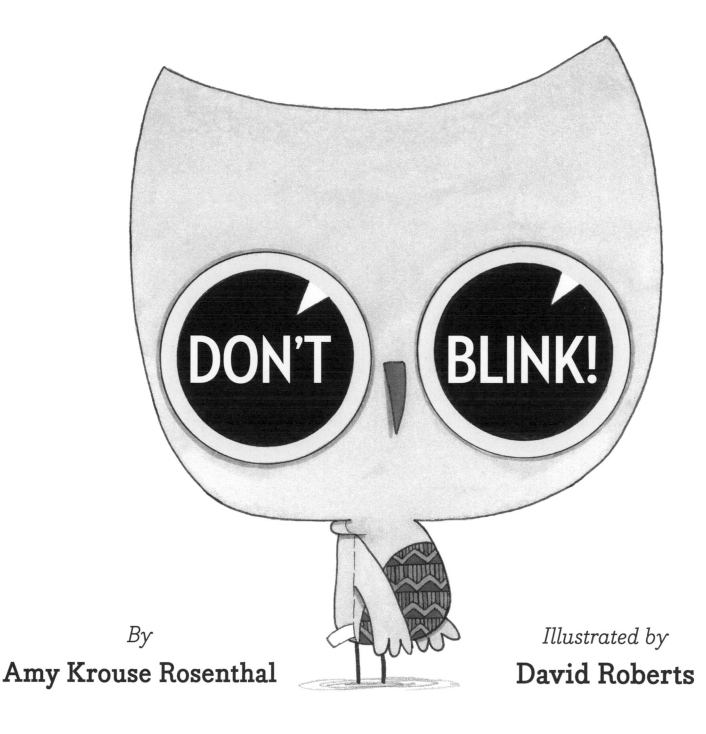

DON'T BLINK!

By
Amy Krouse Rosenthal

Illustrated by
David Roberts

Random House 🏠 New York

Here's how it works:

If you can avoid getting to the end of this book,
you can avoid bedtime, simple as that.

(It's a pretty sweet deal, actually.)

But each time you

2

NK you have to turn a page.

Those are just the rules. So whatever you do,

DO NOT BLINK!

Okay, maybe I wasn't clear enough. Each and every time you

BLINK

you will have to turn the page.

So I repeat:

NO BLINKING!

JEEPERS!

You **BLINKED** again!

I thought you wanted to stay awake!
You do realize that each **BLINK**
gets you closer to you-know-what?!

TRY NOT TO BLINK!

Now I'm just plain confused. Do you want to stay up or not?

Think of it this way: the opposite of

BLINKING

is

STARING.

Try . . . I don't know . . . STARING up at the ceiling.

I should have suggested something more interesting.

STARE at the person next to you.

I guess not interesting enough. (No offense, Person.)

Here. **STARE** at this picture. How many legs do you see?

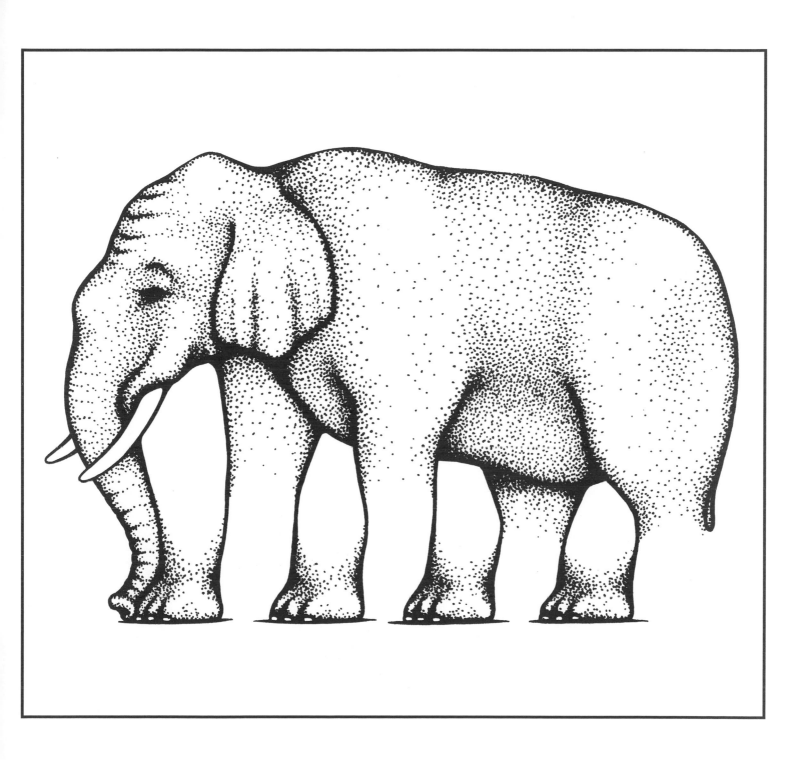

As fun as that was, you obviously still

So let's take this in a slightly different direction.
STARE at this. Amazing, right?
(I don't get how it works, either!)

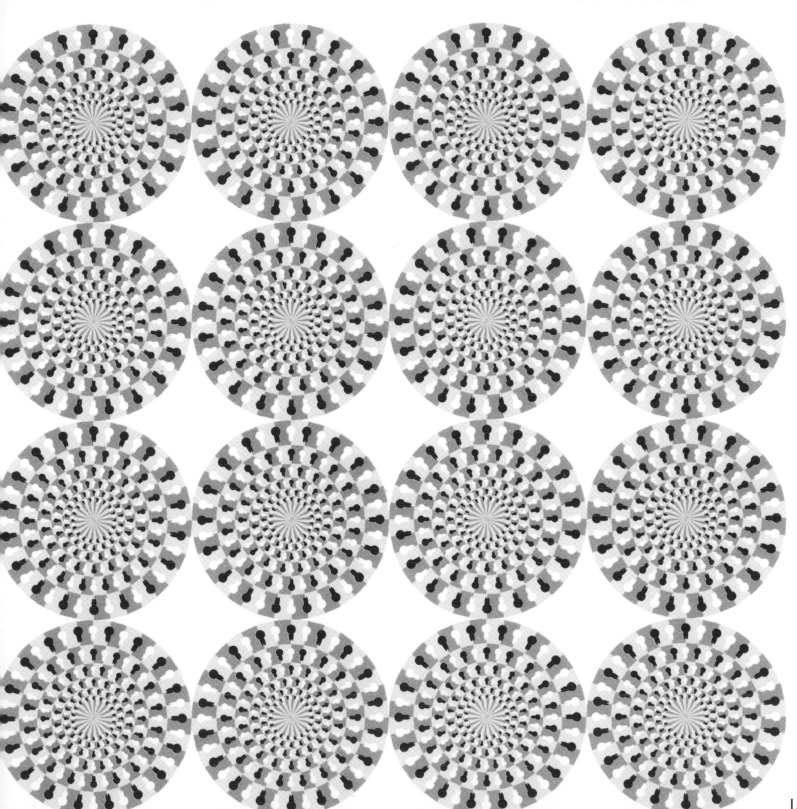

15

Okay, the **STARING** thing is clearly not working.

Maybe **SQUINTING** is the way to go.

Pretend the sun is making you **SQUINT.**

Might that keep you from **BLINKING?**

Nope.

That didn't help. It only made things

BLURRY.

All right. Stay calm. We'll figure this out together.

I know! How about covering one eye?

Dang! You still BLINKED the other eye.

Think. Think. How not to BLINK?

How about using your fingers to hold your eyes open?

Well, that seems to have bought you a few extra seconds.

But we still need a better plan. Hmmm.

Maybe try getting all your **BLINKING** out.

BLINK a whole bunch of times *SUPER FAST!*

Oooh, sorry, baaaaaad idea. That made us jump ahead so many pages we basically time-traveled.

BLINK
BLINK
BLINK
BLINK
BLINK
BLINK

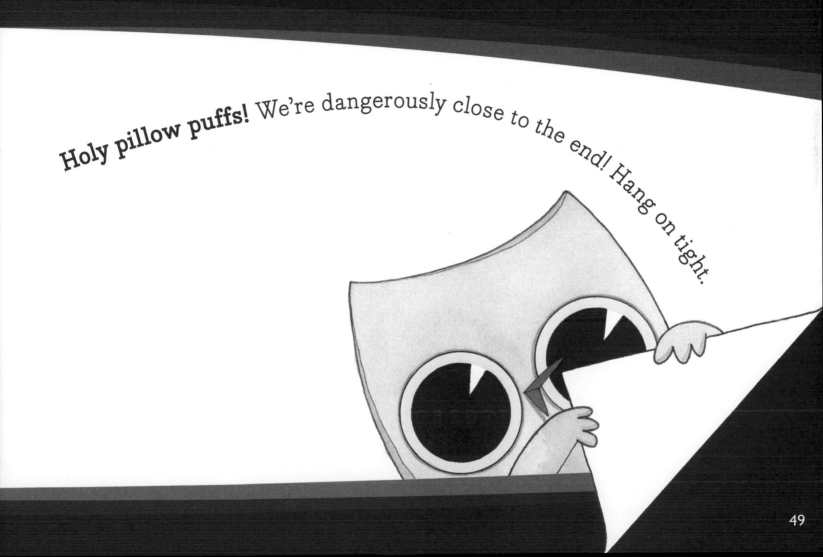

Holy pillow puffs! We're dangerously close to the end! Hang on tight.

The only thing I can come up with is to just close both eyes. At least then you won't be

BLINKING! And we won't have to turn the page. And you avoid bedtime!

So go ahead and close your eyes.

Keep them nice and closed.

You can think about your day.

You can hum your favorite song.

You can count to one million.

Just whatever you do,

DON'T FALL ASLEEP!

But if you do fall asleep, don't worry because it will be morning again . . .

. . . in the BLINK of an eye.